Hovering with Henry

Hovering with Henry

Dora Thatcher

Drawings by Biro

BROCKHAMPTON PRESS

ISBN 0 340 16572 3

First published 1961 by
Brockhampton Press Ltd, Salisbury Road, Leicester
Second impression 1972
Printed in Great Britain by C. Tinling & Co. Ltd, Prescot
Text copyright © 1961 Dora Thatcher
Illustrations copyright © 1961 Brockhampton Press

Contents

Henry's air display

HENRY is a cheerful little helicopter. He has a shining red body, three white wheels, and a set of silvery rotor blades like the sails of a windmill. He shares a hangar with his friends Bumps the charter plane, Ferdie the big freighter, and Clarence the cargo plane.

The aerodrome outside the hangar is a very exciting place. Henry spends many happy hours when he isn't working, watching air liners landing and taking off. But, most of the time, Henry is very busy ferrying especially important people, or fetching especially important packages, or just helping folks in trouble. Sometimes he goes to the mountains. Sometimes he goes to the sea. Sometimes he goes to the big town.

One morning he was outside his hangar watching Ferdie being loaded. Sam, Henry's pilot, came running across the grass. He carried a small box.

'I want you to fly as fast as you can this morning, Henry,' he called. He climbed into Henry's cabin and started his engine.

'What's the matter?' asked Henry.

'One of the big air liners has just brought this package from far away over the sea,' explained Sam. 'It's special medicine for a little boy who is very ill.'

'Where do we have to take it?' asked Henry.

'The boy lives beside the school in the little village among the mountains,' replied Sam. 'You can land in the school playground.'

Henry flew as fast as he could towards the mountains. Presently he saw the thatched roofs of the little village, and the grey school tower with a bell in it. As soon as he touched down in the yard, red uniforms was practising near the aerodrome office. All morning special jet planes kept arriving to take part in the display. Ferdie and Clarence were standing proudly on the grass outside the hangar. Bumps was waiting near the end of the runway. Henry was in a special rope enclosure. Sam had printed a large card, which said:

HELICOPTER FLIGHTS
50p
Children - Half price
TAKE A TRIP AND HELP
THE HOSPITAL

Just before lunch the man from the aerodrome office came to the enclosure.

'What do you think, Sam?' he shouted. 'Prince Tamari is on holiday here from India. He's coming to the air display.'

'A real prince!' exclaimed Henry.

'He's very rich,' explained Sam. 'Perhaps you'll be able to take him for two rides, Henry.'

Straight after lunch lots of people began to arrive. Presently a long silver sports car drove up to the aerodrome gates. In it was Prince Tamari. The aerodrome controller hurried to meet him, and the band played a special tune. Henry watched the prince. He wore an ordinary suit, just like Sam, but on his head was a snowy-white turban. Fastened in front of it, flashing like a red flame, was an enormous jewel.

'That's the famous Indian Star Ruby,' whispered Sam. 'It's very valuable.'

Prince Tamari did enjoy the display. He watched the jet planes do their dangerous tricks. He went right inside Ferdie and Clarence. He took a trip with Bumps, and he threw balls at the coconuts.

But Henry was so busy taking people for flights that he hadn't time to watch anything. The bag of money in Sam's pocket grew heavier and heavier.

'Keep it up,' chuckled Sam. 'We're doing splendidly.'

'Have we made the five thousand pounds yet?' asked Henry.

'Not yet,' said Sam. 'But we're getting on very well. Oh, here comes Prince Tamari. Would you like a helicopter flight, sir?'

'Yes, I would indeed,' boomed Prince Tamari. 'I like helicopters. I've two of my own in India.'

He climbed into Henry's cabin. Sam started the engine, and up went Henry.

'Do you think I could pilot him?' asked the prince.

'Of course you may,' replied Sam willingly.

Prince Tamari sat behind Henry's controls. He soared upwards and he dropped downwards until poor Henry felt rather giddy. But the prince really enjoyed himself.

'Thank you very much, Henry,' he said when they were safely on the ground. 'Here's five pounds, Sam. Henry is a splendid little helicopter. Now I'm afraid I must go.'

Henry's next passenger was a very plump lady. Sam was just trying to ease her through the cabin door when the aerodrome controller hurried up.

'Henry!' he shouted. 'The prince has lost the Indian Star. Do have a look in your cabin.'

Sam searched every corner, but the big ruby wasn't there. The air display announcer told the crowd over the radio that the prince would give one thousand pounds reward to the person who returned the ruby to him. So everyone started to search. No one wanted roundabout, plane or helicopter rides.

'I do hope it's found soon,' said Henry. 'Otherwise we won't raise the money that Doctor Smith needs.'

But it wasn't! Evening came. The prince left and everyone else went home. The special jet planes took off for their own aerodromes. The coconut shies were pulled down. The band put away their instruments. Ferdie, Clarence and Bumps were towed into their hangars.

'Before we go to bed we'll take the money we collected to Doctor Smith,' said Sam.

'Did we get enough?' asked Henry.

'No,' sighed Sam. 'But perhaps we can think of some other way of raising the rest. It was a very good idea of yours, Henry.'

Sam jumped into Henry's cabin and started his engine.

'Up we go,' he cried.

But Henry's rotor blades wouldn't turn.

'Come on, Henry,' coaxed Sam. 'It'll be dark soon.'

'I can't,' protested Henry. 'There's something wrong.'

Sam fetched his tool kit from Henry's tail and

quickly set to work to unfasten some screws.

'Well, I don't—' he began. 'Goodness! There's something wedging your lever. Henry! It's the Indian Star! It must have dropped down while the prince was piloting you.'

'Well, bless my rotors!' exclaimed Henry.

'We'd better take it back straight away,' said Sam. 'The prince is staying in a hotel near the railway station in the big town. We'll call there on our way up to see Doctor Smith.'

Henry landed in the station yard. Sam hurried to the large hotel nearby. Henry waited. Presently Sam came back. Prince Tamari was with him.

'I had to come and say "Thank you," Henry,' said the prince. 'It would have been dreadful if the Ruby had really been lost. Here is your reward.'

He handed Sam a piece of paper with writing on it. It was a cheque for one thousand pounds.

'Reward!' exclaimed Henry. 'But I didn't really find it.'

'Oh, yes you did,' said the prince. 'I promised one thousand pounds to the person who returned it to me.'

'Sam!' cried Henry. 'Can we give it to Doctor Smith?'

'That's just what I was going to

suggest,' laughed Sam. 'With the money we've already collected, Doctor Smith will be able to have his new hospital wing.'

A few months later, Bobby, now quite well again, went with Henry and Sam to see the official opening of the new wing. Henry had a real surprise. Over the doorway he saw in bold black letters:

'HENRY'S WING'

Underneath was a carving of a helicopter just like himself.

Henry and Choo-Choo

'WE'RE going to the railway station in the big town,' said Sam one fine spring morning. 'There's a special parcel for collection.'

'Oh, I like going to the railway station,' cried Henry. 'There's always something happening.'

Sam started his engines, and up went Henry. Soon he was dropping slowly down into the yard beside the station. Sam went into the parcels office. Henry looked around him.

'Parp! Parp! Good morning, Henry,' called a taxi who was waiting for a passenger.

'Good morning,' replied Henry politely.

'Honk! Honk!' went a railway van, who was being loaded with packing cases. 'Good morning, Henry. It's nice to see you again.'

'Good morning,' replied Henry politely.

All at once he heard a faint whistle far away.

'Here comes Choo-Choo, the mountain engine,' said the railway van, who knew the times of every train.

Chuff-chuff-chuff. Alongside the platform drew a little blue engine towing four red carriages and a guard's van behind it.

Henry peeped over the railings. 'Good-morning, Choo-choo,' he called cheerily.

'Why, it's Henry,' whistled the little blue engine. 'We haven't seen you for such a long time.'

'What have you been doing?' added his driver, whose name was William.

'Lots of things,' said Henry.

Just then Sam came out of the parcels office.

'Sam,' called William. 'I know you like birds.'

'Yes,' agreed Sam. 'I like taking pictures of them. I've got a splendid new camera.'

'We were going up the hill towards Mountain End Station,' explained William, 'when I saw the biggest bird I've ever seen up on the rocks above us.'

'What did it look like?' asked Sam.

'It was a sort of golden brown,' said William. 'I

think it had a blackish hooked beak with yellow markings. It had simply enormous wings.'

'It sounds like a golden eagle,' cried Sam excitedly. 'I'd heard that they'd been seen in the mountains.'

'Perhaps it was,' said William. 'Why don't you go and have a look, Sam? Henry could take you.'

'We simply must find out,' cried Sam. 'We'll go as soon as we've finished work today. I wonder if it's building a nest.'

'Come along, Choo-Choo,' said William. 'It's time we went.'

'Goodbye, Henry,' called Choo-Choo. 'I go up to Mountain End Station again this evening. Perhaps I'll see you.'

'I hope so,' said Henry.

'Choo-Choo!' whistled Choo-Choo. Chuff-chuff-chuff. Away went the four red carriages and the guard's van.

'We'd better go too, Henry,' called Sam. 'We must hurry so that we finish our work early.'

After tea Sam fetched his binoculars and his new camera. He filled Henry's tank with petrol and they set off.

They flew towards the mountains, and presently they were in the twisty valley that led to Mountain End Station. The valley got narrower and narrower, with steep rocky slopes on either side.

'Can you see the golden eagle?' asked Henry.

'Not yet,' replied Sam. 'Keep looking, Henry. I wouldn't want to miss it.'

Henry looked and looked. 'What's that over there?' he asked suddenly.

A bird with enormous wings was gliding near the top of the cliffs.

'That's it!' shouted Sam. 'It *is* a golden eagle. Oh Henry, this is exciting!'

Henry flew as quietly as he could up the valley. Sam looked through his binoculars.

'I think there may be a nest on the ledge about half-way up,' he cried. 'I can see some sticks. I must take a photograph of it.'

But most of the nest was hidden behind a tangled bush. Sam *was* disappointed.

'I'll put you down on that little patch of grass just above the railway line,' he said. 'Then I can climb up the rocks and take a picture.'

Henry went slowly down until his little white wheels rested on the grass. A gentle slope ran down to the railway line.

'I won't be long,' said Sam.

He climbed out of the cabin. He put his camera and binoculars round his neck and started to climb up the steep rocks. The golden eagle still glided in the sky overhead.

Very carefully Sam clambered upwards. Henry watched. The golden eagle watched too. Sam reached a ledge near the nest. He took off his

camera and opened it. The golden eagle dropped lower. Sam pressed the button. All at once the golden eagle swooped down-wards.

Sam was so startled that he dropped his precious camera. It rolled over the edge. It hung by its strap on a stunted bush below the ledge.

'Careful, Sam!' shouted Henry, as Sam stretched out to reach it. 'Do be careful!'

But his warning came too late. The rock broke away. Sam slithered and rolled down the cliff. A big rock tumbled and bounced after him.

'Sam!' yelled Henry in alarm. 'Are you hurt?'

24

For a few moments there was no answer.

'Sam!' shouted Henry again. 'Sam!'

'I think I'm all right,' came Sam's voice. 'But this rock is pressing against my leg, and I can't move.'

'Don't worry,' called Henry. 'I'll get help.'

But suddenly he remembered that without Sam to start his engines, he couldn't fly. He looked all around him. But there was no one to be seen. Henry *was* worried. Whatever could he do to help Sam?

All at once, from far down the valley, he heard a faint whistle. Choo-Choo! William would help

Sam. But suppose Choo-Choo didn't stop. He was pulling a heavy train up a steep hill. His pistons would be making so much noise that perhaps he wouldn't hear Henry call.

Henry wriggled and waggled and jerked. Slowly, his little white wheels began to run down the slope. Faster and faster he ran, until he was standing right across the railway line.

Nearer came the chuffing sound. A little plume of white smoke appeared in the air. Choo-Choo was getting very close. Suddenly the little blue engine appeared round the bend. He *was* going fast. Suppose he couldn't stop in time! Poor Henry closed his eyes and waited. There was a screech of brakes. When he opened them again, Choo-Choo's buffer was almost touching his nose.

'Why, Henry,' he scolded. 'You silly little helicopter. Whatever are you doing in the middle of my lines? I might have run into you and smashed you to pieces.'

'I'm sorry, Choo-Choo,' said Henry. 'But Sam fell down the rocks. He's lying up there with one of them pressing on his leg, and he can't get up.'

'Oh dear!' cried William. 'We'd better go and help him.'

He climbed down from his driving cabin. The guard climbed out of his van. The passengers climbed out of the red carriages. They all tried to move the rock that was pressing on Sam's leg. But it was no use.

'Perhaps I could lift it,' suggested Henry.

'It's much too heavy,' replied William. 'And if you dropped it, you might hurt Sam badly.'

'We *must* get him out,' sobbed Henry.

'Don't worry, old chap,' called William. 'We'll think of a way.'

Everyone thought and thought. Suddenly Henry had an idea.

'I know how to help Sam,' he exclaimed. 'If we all work together, I'm sure we can lift the rock just enough to free him.'

'How can we do it?' asked William.

'Lying on the ground beside the railway line is a new telegraph-pole,' explained Henry. 'Will you bring it up here, and push one end under the edge of the rock?'

William and the guard and the passengers dragged the big telegraph-pole up the slope, and did as Henry asked.

'Now what shall we do?' asked William.

'First, loop the strong wire rope from my winch

round the rock,' ordered Henry. 'Then climb into my cabin and start my engine, please.'

William did so.

'Now, if you'll drive me,' explained Henry, 'I'm going up a little way. When I waggle my rotors, I want the guard and all the passengers to press down as hard as they can on the other end of the telegraph-pole.'

'Just like a see-saw,' exclaimed William. 'You *are* clever.'

Henry went up, and William started his winch. Henry waggled his rotors. The guard and the passengers pressed down on the telegraph-pole. Henry pulled on the rope as hard as he could.

The rock was very heavy. But suddenly it lifted just a little. In a flash Sam had pulled his leg free.

'I'm out,' he shouted. 'Thank you, Henry. You can land again now.'

William climbed out of Henry's cabin.

'Are you sure you're all right, Sam?' asked Henry.

'Just a little cut and a bruise on my leg,' replied Sam. 'Thank you all very much. Why, I haven't even broken my camera. I'm sure I'll have a wonderful picture of the golden eagle's nest.'

'Then we'd better be getting along,' said William. 'Come on, Choo-Choo. Best steam up. We're late.'

'Goodbye, Henry,' called Choo-Choo. 'See you another day.'

'Goodbye, Choo-Choo,' replied Henry.

Sam started Henry's engine. As they went up they could see the little blue engine chuffing into Mountain End Station. Then they turned back down the valley towards their own aerodrome.

Henry and sheep-dog Lass

SAM was climbing into Henry's cabin one morning when suddenly a mud-spattered truck raced across the grass towards them. It stopped with a jerk. A red-faced farmer in wellingtons and an old jacket jumped out.

'Phew!' he panted. 'I nearly missed you. Are you going over High Tor Farm today, Henry?'

'Yes, we are,' replied Sam.

'We often go that way,' added Henry.

'Splendid!' cried the farmer. 'Could you deliver a message to Farmer Robbins for me? His telephone is out of order.'

'Of course we will,' said Sam. 'He's a great friend of ours.'

'Will you tell him that the time of the sheep-dog trials tomorrow has been changed from quarter past two to twelve o'clock?' explained the farmer.

31

'Sheep-dog trials!' exclaimed Henry. 'Whatever are those?'

'A competition to find the best sheep-dog,' said the man. 'Farmer Robbins has a wonderful dog. She won the silver cup last year. I wouldn't like her to miss the competition.'

'She won't,' laughed Sam. 'We'll tell Farmer Robbins.'

'Thank you very much,' said the farmer.

Sam started Henry's engines and off they went towards the mountains. Up and up until at last, in the middle of the wide lonely moor, there was the old grey farmhouse. Henry sank gently down beside the duck pond.

Farmer Robbins came out of the barn. A black and white dog with a waving feathery tail followed him.

'Hello, Henry,' he called. 'It is nice of you to visit us.'

'We can't stay,' said Sam. 'We just came to tell you that the time of the sheep-dog trials has been changed to twelve o'clock.'

'Thank you very much,' said Farmer Robbins.

'We wouldn't want to miss that, would we, Lass?'

The black and white dog pushed her nose into his hand and licked it gently.

'Is that the dog who won the silver cup?' asked Henry.

'Yes,' said Farmer Robbins proudly.

Lass wagged her tail.

'I wish I could see her win,' sighed Henry. 'I've never seen a sheep-dog trial.'

'We'll see how much work we have to do,' laughed Sam. 'Now we'd better be on our way, or we'll never be finished today.'

'Goodbye,' shouted Farmer Robbins. 'Thank you very much for bringing the message.'

'Good luck, Lass,' called Henry.

The very next morning Henry had to take a most important passenger to a big town the other side of the mountains. On the way back he passed near High Tor Farm.

'I expect Farmer Robbins has already gone to the sheep-dog trials,' said Sam.

'Then who is that?' asked Henry. 'Look! On top of that little hill waving a red handkerchief.'

Sam peered out of his cabin. 'Gracious! It's Farmer Robbins. We'd better see what he wants.'

Henry went down gently on to a grassy space on top of the hill.

'What's the matter?' called Sam.

'It's Lass!' replied Farmer Robbins. 'I sent her to bring in some sheep this morning, and she hasn't come back.'

'Perhaps she found a rabbit to chase,' suggested Sam.

'Not my Lass,' said Farmer Robbins proudly. 'She's the most obedient dog in the world. Did you see her when you came over the mountains?'

'No,' answered Sam. 'We'll go and look for her. You'd better come with us. You can watch for her while I steer Henry. It's rather dangerous to fly low among these hills.'

'Thank you very much,' said Farmer Robbins. He climbed up into Henry's cabin, and up they went.

Henry flew slowly to and fro just above the coarse yellowish grass.

'Baa-baa!' cried the black-faced sheep as he passed over them.

But there was no trace of the black and white dog.

Farmer Robbins *was* worried. 'She must be hurt,' he cried. 'Whatever shall I do?'

Suddenly, grazing near some twisted bushes, Henry saw two shaggy brown mountain ponies. 'There's Star and Prince, Sam,' he cried excitedly. 'Perhaps they've seen Lass.'

Star, the mare with the white, star-shaped mark

on her forehead, whinnied when she saw Henry. Her colt, Prince, trotted timidly nearer his mother.

'Are you looking for something, Henry?' neighed Star.

'Yes,' replied Henry. 'Lass, the black and white sheep-dog is lost.'

'I saw her early this morning,' replied Star. 'She was driving some sheep near the Castle Rocks on the other side of the moor.'

The Castle Rocks were three great crags, tumbled on the hillside like a giant's house. Henry hovered over them. Farmer Robbins and Sam peered out.

'You'd better land on that small flat space on top of the rocks, Henry,' said Sam.

Henry went nervously down. There was barely room for his three white wheels. All around him were steep cliffs. He did hope the wind wouldn't blow him over the edge. Sam stopped his engine.

'Lass! Lass!' shouted Farmer Robbins.

They all listened hard, but there was only the trilling of a lark high in the sky.

'Lass! Lass!' shouted Farmer Robbins again.

Suddenly, from far away among the rocks, came a faint barking.

'It's her!' exclaimed Farmer Robbins. He and Sam scrambled away in the direction of the sound. Henry waited. Minutes passed.

Then Sam came back. 'We've found her,' he called, 'but she's slipped into a gully. We can't climb down to her because the rock slopes inwards, and it's breaking away. We need you to hold a rope for us, Henry.'

Sam jumped into Henry's cabin and started his engines. Henry went up over the rocks until he could see Farmer Robbins standing on the edge of the gully. Sam let down the rope ladder. Farmer Robbins climbed on to it. 'Ready!' he called.

Gently, gently, Henry lowered the ladder down into the gully. He knew he must keep the ladder steady, or Farmer Robbins would crash against the rocks. It *was* difficult.

It seemed hours before Farmer Robbins signalled to be pulled up. But at last there he was, safe and sound on the end of the ladder, with Lass in his arms.

'Is she hurt?' asked Henry when they were back in his cabin.

'Not a scratch,' laughed Farmer Robbins. 'She must have rolled. Well, we've missed the sheep-dog trials, old girl. But I don't mind as long as you are safe.'

'What time is it?' asked Henry, having an idea.

'A quarter to two,' replied Sam.

'If they started at twelve o'clock, all the other dogs will have had their turns by two o'clock,' explained Farmer Robbins. 'If Lass isn't there when the last dog has finished, she can't enter.'

'If I fly as fast as I can, perhaps I can get there in time,' suggested Henry.

'It's quite a long way. . . ' began Sam doubtfully.

'Please let me try,' begged Henry.

'All right,' laughed Sam.

Up shot Henry like a jet propelled rocket, and away he went as fast as he could go. Across the moor, over the farmhouse, down the mountain he roared.

'How much longer?' he panted.

'Four minutes,' yelled Sam.

'There's the field,' cried Farmer Robbins excitedly.

Henry could see crowds of people, a flock of sheep, and a large white tent.

'Two minutes!' shouted Sam. 'Hurry, Henry!'

Henry raced towards the field. He dropped down on the grass right beside the tent. Farmer Robbins jumped out and hurried into the tent just as the hands on Sam's watch pointed to two o'clock.

'Well done, Henry!' laughed Sam.

A few moments later Farmer Robbins came out of the tent. 'Thank you very much, Henry. Lass is to take her test straight away.'

'Please, Sam, can we stay and watch her?' pleaded Henry.

'All right then,' agreed Sam.

He pushed Henry into a good spot beside the ropes.

'You must be very quiet,' he added, 'or Lass won't hear Farmer Robbins's signals.'

'I will,' whispered Henry.

Farmer Robbins bent down and spoke to Lass. Like a black and white arrow she raced to the top of the field where five sheep were grazing. Quickly but carefully Lass gathered them together and began to drive them towards two gates set up in the middle of the field. Now and again Farmer

Robbins gave a special whistle. Lass obeyed him instantly. Sometimes she dropped down on the ground. Sometimes she wheeled to one side. Everyone was very quiet.

Lass drove the sheep between the gates. Then at another signal she separated one from the other four. Then she drove them safely into a pen beside Farmer Robbins.

Everyone clapped and clapped. Farmer Robbins and Lass came back to where Henry was waiting.

'Lass was wonderful,' cried Henry.

'How did you teach her to do that?' asked Sam.

'Just patience,' laughed Farmer Robbins. 'She didn't make a single mistake.' He patted the silky black head proudly.

'Has she won the silver cup?' asked Henry.

'We shall know in a few moments,' replied Farmer Robbins.

All at once the loud-speaker outside the tent started to crackle. Then the announcer spoke.

'Event No. 10. Winner of the Silver Championship Cup – Lass. Owned and trained by Farmer Robbins.'

Everyone cheered and waved their arms.

'She's won!' yelled Henry.

'Good old Lass!' added Sam.

'It's really thanks to you, Henry,' said Farmer Robbins. 'If you hadn't found her and brought her here in time, she wouldn't have been able to enter.'

'That's all right,' said Henry. 'It was fun.'

'Goodness gracious!' exclaimed Sam. 'Talking of time, we were due back at the aerodrome half an hour ago. Come along, Henry. Best rotor forward.'

Sam jumped into the cabin and started the engines. Up shot Henry.

'Goodbye, and thank you,' shouted Farmer Robbins.

'Wuff-wuff!' barked Lass.

Henry flew back towards the aerodrome as fast as he could go.

Rum Tum's new home

RUM TUM, Henry's friend, was a cement mixer. He had a round bowl of a body and a rumbly tumbly voice. He was such a jolly mixer that everyone liked him.

One day Rum Tum was brought to the aerodrome to help make a new runway. Henry *was* pleased. He liked to hear Rum Tum's rumbling voice when he woke up in the morning. He liked to tell Rum Tum all about his adventures when they'd both finished work for the day.

But one morning there was no cheerful rumbling to wake Henry up.

'Has Rum Tum gone away, Sam?' he asked.

'No,' replied Sam. 'He's still outside. But he's getting rather old and slow. So they've brought a special new machine to make the runway.'

Sam pushed Henry out of the hangar and went

off to the aerodrome office. Rum Tum was standing on the grass nearby.

'Hello, Rum Tum,' called Henry cheerfully. 'I hear you're going to have a nice rest.'

'I don't want a rest,' sobbed Rum Tum. 'I like mixing cement. But they've brought a special new machine. They don't need me any more. Whatever will become of me now?'

'I'm sure they'll find a job for you soon,' said Henry comfortingly.

But they didn't. All day long Rum Tum stood empty and neglected outside the hangar. His round bowl body began to rust. His jolly rumbling tumbling voice was silent.

'Poor Rum Tum,' said Henry one evening, as Sam was putting him back into the hangar. 'I do wish they'd let him mix cement again. He's so unhappy.'

'It is a pity,' agreed Sam. 'But he *is* rather slow.'

Sam went away and Henry dozed. Suddenly he was awakened by a huge clap of thunder. The rain beat on the roof, the wind screamed round the walls and great flashes of lightning lit up the

hangar. Not
one of the
planes got a
wink of sleep
all night.

'What a
dreadful
night,'
grumbled
Ferdie the
freighter plane next morning.

Henry yawned. Suddenly the hangar door
opened and in came Sam.

'Come along, Henry,' he called cheerily. 'We've
an urgent job to do.'

'Oh dear! I'm so tired,' complained Henry.

'I'm sorry, but I'm afraid we must go,' said Sam.
'The rain last night flooded the road to Marshfield
Farm. The railway van has some boxes of baby
chicks to deliver to Mr Brown, and it can't get
through the water.'

'Baby chicks!' exclaimed Henry.

'Yes,' replied Sam. 'They must be taken out of

45

their boxes at once, or they'll die. So I've promised we'll take them.'

A soft 'cheep–cheep' came from the six boxes as the driver of the railway van and Sam loaded them into Henry's cabin. Sam started Henry's engines and off they went.

'Which way do we go?' asked Henry.

'Over the wide river and the big town,' explained Sam. 'Marshfield is the big chicken farm on that flat ground right on the edge of the sea.'

It was still raining and the wind was still blowing very hard as Henry flew towards the seaside.

'It's hard work flying against this wind,' he panted.

'We're nearly there,' said Sam. 'You can see the red roof of the farmhouse over there.'

Henry dropped down into the yard beside a big shed. Sam climbed down and knocked at the door of the farmhouse. There was no reply.

'He can't be far away,' said Sam. 'Perhaps he's feeding his chickens. Let's go and see.'

He climbed back into Henry's cabin and they flew slowly over the fields. They found Mr Brown near the wall that divided his field from the beach. He was struggling to lift a small hen house.

'Good morning,' called Sam. 'We've brought some boxes of chicks for you. The road was flooded and the railway van couldn't get through.'

'Thank you,' replied Mr Brown, mopping his forehead with his handkerchief. 'It's not the only place that was flooded either.'

'Why?' asked Sam.

'The sea tore a great hole in my wall last night,' explained Mr Brown. 'It washed away two of my hen houses. So I'm moving the smaller ones to the high ground nearer the house.'

'Can Henry help you move them?' asked Sam.

'Thank you very much,' said Mr Brown.

He and Sam put ropes round the smaller hen houses, and Henry carried them up to the field beside the farmhouse. At last only two very large solid ones were left.

'If the tide is very high this evening, those will be washed away too, I'm afraid,' sighed Mr Brown. 'But they're much too big to move.'

'Can't you mend the hole in the wall?' asked Henry.

'There isn't time,' explained Mr Brown. 'The tide will be up in five hours. I'll pile up a few stones, but the waves are very strong. If only we had a cement mixer and some bags of special quick-drying cement, we might save the big hen houses.'

'Cement mixer!' exclaimed Henry. 'There's Rum Tum. He'll help you. I know he will.'

'Who's Rum Tum?' asked Mr Brown.

'He's an old cement mixer rusting away on our aerodrome,' explained Sam. 'There are some bags of quick-drying cement there, too.'

'But the roads are flooded. How can we get him here?' asked Mr Brown.

'I'll bring him,' cried Henry. 'Do hurry and start my engine, Sam. We'd better go straight away.'

Henry flew as fast as he could back to the aerodrome.

'Rum Tum!' he shouted as soon as his three little white wheels touched the ground. 'We've got a job for you.'

49

'For me?' croaked Rum Tum, rusty-voiced.

'Yes,' answered Henry. 'There's a big hole in the sea wall at Marshfield Farm. They need you to mix cement to stop it up before the tide comes in and washes away some more chicken houses.'

'Oh, I'll work as fast as I can,' rumbled Rum Tum excitedly.

Sam hurried away towards the aerodrome office. Presently he came back with six bags of cement on a cart. He loaded them into Henry's cabin.

'Now you, Rum Tum,' he cried.

He fastened some ropes round the old cement mixer. Henry went up until he was right over Rum Tum. The ropes were attached to his cabin.

'Steady now, Henry,' called Sam.

Very gently Henry began to rise. He flew steadily towards the seaside, with Rum Tum dangling beneath him. He was rather heavy, but at last they were going down again into the field beside the sea wall.

As soon as Rum Tum was safely on the ground Mr Brown filled up his round bowl with stones and sand, tipped in a bag of cement and started his engine.

'Rumble-tumble-rumble,' went Rum Tum.

'Splish-splosh-splash,' went the stones and sand and cement.

Mr Brown piled stones into the hole, and as soon as it was ready the cement was poured and patted into place.

Henry was busy too. He helped put some of the heavier stones into position. Then he flew to and fro from the beach to the field with loads of rocks and buckets of sand.

The waves came higher and higher up the beach behind the wall.

'Hurry, Rum Tum!' shouted Mr Brown.

Rum Tum rumbled faster than ever. Out came another load of mixed cement. Henry flew back with more sand and stones. Into Rum Tum's round body it went with another bag of cement.

'Nearly finished,' panted Mr Brown. 'Henry, could you move this stone for me?'

Henry heaved another great rock into place. Mr Brown slapped some more cement round it.

Just as the first wave touched the other side of the wall, he set the last stones in the hole with the last shovelful of cement.

'Well done, Rum Tum,' cried Henry.

'Thank you very much, Henry, Sam and Rum Tum,' said Mr Brown gratefully. 'You've saved my chicken houses.'

'It was good fun racing the sea,' chuckled Henry.

'I enjoyed every minute of it,' rumbled Rum Tum. 'I love mixing cement.'

'You're a very good mixer too,' said Mr Brown. 'I wish I could keep you.'

'I'm sure they'd be willing to sell him very cheaply,' explained Sam. 'He was only rusting away on the aerodrome.'

'Please let me stay,' pleaded Rum Tum.

52

'Well, there's always work for a good cement mixer on a chicken farm, and I can lend you to my farmer friends as well,' said Mr Brown. 'I'll go and telephone the aerodrome straight away and see what they say.'

He hurried off into the house. While they all waited Sam polished some of the rust off Rum Tum's engine with a piece of rag.

In a few moments Mr Brown came back.

'It's all settled. I've bought you, Rum Tum,' he called cheerily.

'Hurrah!' rumbled Rum Tum. 'I've got a new home.'

'And I know you'll be happy here,' said Henry. 'We'll be able to come and see him when we're flying this way, won't we, Sam?'

'Of course we will,' said Sam. 'And now we must go home too.'

Henry was so tired after his sleepless night and all the hard work, that he couldn't even stay awake long enough to tell Ferdie about Rum Tum's new home. As soon as Sam pushed him into the hangar he fell fast asleep.

Henry's busy holiday

IT was very hot. As Henry stood on the grass outside his hangar his red body felt scorched and his little white wheels smelt sticky and rubbery. Sam came across the grass from the aerodrome office.

'Phew!' he said, mopping his forehead with a large white handkerchief. 'It's too hot to work today.'

'Have we to do any special jobs?' asked Henry.

'No,' replied Sam. 'It's Saturday. So we'll have a whole day's holiday.'

'Can't we go somewhere cool?' panted Henry. 'My hangar is very stuffy, and I'm sure my tyres will melt if I stay here.'

'We'll go to the seaside,' decided Sam. 'I'll have a bathe and you can paddle your wheels in the sea. That will cool down your tyres.'

'That's a wonderful idea!' exclaimed Henry. 'I like the seaside.'

He waited while Sam went to fetch his bathing costume and towel, a packet of sandwiches and a bottle of lemonade.

Just then Ferdie the freighter plane came out of the hangar.

'Where are you going today, Henry?' he asked.

'To the seaside,' answered Henry. 'We've got a day's holiday.'

'You are lucky,' grumbled Ferdie. 'I shall be busy all day.'

As soon as Sam came back he started Henry's engine and up they went.

'Which seaside are we going to?' asked Henry.

'There's a special little bay a few miles down the coast,' explained Sam. 'It shouldn't be too crowded. The roads leading to it are rather narrow, but that won't bother us, will it?'

'No, it won't,' chuckled Henry.

They passed over the big town and the shining silver river. A fussy little tugboat was pulling a string of barges.

'Where are you going, Henry?' he tootled.

'To the seaside,' replied Henry. 'We're having a holiday today.'

They passed over the dockside with its row of tall cranes.

'Where are you going, Henry?' hooted a big steamer beside the quay.

'To the seaside,' replied Henry. 'We're having a holiday today.'

'You are lucky,' said the big steamer.

'It isn't far now,' said Sam as they flew over the fields towards the cliffs. 'Look, there's the road that leads to the bay. It's lucky we're up here. What a lot of cars there are.'

'If they're going to the seaside, why aren't they moving?' asked Henry. 'And why are they making all that noise?'

'Perhaps there's something wrong,' said Sam. 'Let's go down a little lower and find out.'

Henry dropped down and flew above the road. There were big cars full of children, and small cars too, all blowing their horns; there was a long red bus going 'parp-parp-parp'; behind it was a motor-bike with a sidecar fastened to it going 'toot-toot'; the driver of a lorry loaded with bottles of pop was playing a tune on his klaxon; an ice-cream van was jingling his bells over and over again.

'What a terrible noise,' shouted Sam. 'Something must be wrong.'

'There's someone waving to us over there,' called Henry. 'Perhaps we can help.'

'It's a policeman,' said Sam. 'We'll go down in the field beside the road and see what he wants.'

The policeman was wheeling a bicycle. He *did* look hot.

'Henry, thank goodness you came along,' he cried. 'We're in a dreadful mess.'

'What's the matter?' asked Sam.

'It's Samson the steam-roller,' explained the policeman. 'He'd been rolling the road. He was just going home when he got too near the hedge. His big front roller is tipped over into the ditch. With all the cars in this narrow road, we can't get a breakdown lorry to him.'

'I don't know whether I can manage a steam-roller,' said Henry doubtfully.

'Do try, please,' said the policeman.

'All right,' agreed Henry.

'I'll show you the way,' said the policeman. He got on his bicycle and pedalled off down the road. Henry flew up and followed him slowly.

Although Samson, the black and green steam-roller, was such a big fellow, he wasn't very brave.

'I shall never get out,' he sobbed. 'I shall stick in this ditch until I rust away.'

'Don't be silly,' scolded Henry. 'I'll help you. When I lift, go backwards as hard as you can. We'll soon have you out.'

The policeman and Samson's driver fastened a rope round the frame of the big roller, and then to Henry's winch. Up went Henry.

Samson *was* heavy. He nearly pulled Henry back down again. But slowly, slowly, inch by inch, Henry lifted. 'Quickly!' he panted.

Samson's engine started to pull backwards. Clank-clank-clank! In a few seconds he was safely back on the road again.

'You'd better get inside that field gate and let all this traffic pass,' suggested the policeman. 'Are you very busy, Henry?'

'Well – no —' replied Henry. 'I was only going to the seaside for a day's holiday.'

'Could you stay a little while and help me sort out these cars and lorries?' asked the policeman. 'It takes such a long time on a bicycle, and it's so hot.'

'Of course we will,' laughed Sam. 'Henry's never been a traffic policeman before.'

The policeman climbed into Henry's cabin and they set off slowly above the line of cars. They had stopped blowing their horns and were moving very slowly along the road. All at once a little grey car in the middle of the line stopped again.

'Move along there,' shouted the policeman.

'I can't,' said the little car. 'I've run out of petrol.'

'You silly little car,' scolded the policeman. 'Why —'

'I'll fetch some,' offered Henry. He flew back along the road to the nearest garage and landed beside the pumps. The garage man gave him a canful of petrol and Henry took it to the little grey car. They all started off again, but not for long!

The ice-cream van had a puncture and had forgotten his jack. Henry held him up while they changed his wheel. The driver gave Sam and the policeman a nice cool ice-cream for their help.

Henry fetched a drink of water for a lorry whose engine got too hot. He lifted up a bubble car whose front bumper had locked itself into the back bumper of a large taxi.

By the time the cars were all safely on their way to the seaside it was time for lunch.

'I think we'll have our picnic in that field by the river,' suggested Sam. 'We'll go on to the seaside afterwards.'

'Thank you both very much for your help,' said the policeman. 'We'd never have got them all away without you.'

He rode off on his bicycle and Sam pushed Henry into the shade of a big tree. He ate his sandwiches and drank his lemonade.

'I'll just have a little nap for a few moments,' he said, 'and then we'll go on to the seaside.'

He closed his eyes. Henry dozed too. Suddenly he was awakened by the policeman's voice. 'Henry! Sam!' They both woke up.

'What's the matter?' asked Henry.

'We're in trouble again,' said the policeman.

'More cars?' asked Henry.

'Not this time, but we need your help. Farmer Jones is bringing in his hay from Long Meadow,' explained the policeman. 'The axle on his wagon has just broken and it can't be mended until Monday.'

'Can't the hay wait until Monday?' asked Sam.

'I'm afraid not,' said the policeman. 'The weather man on TV said we might have a thunderstorm. Rain would spoil the hay, so it must be stored today. Could you help to carry it, Henry?'

'All right,' sighed Henry.

'The field is on the other side of the river,'

explained the policeman, preparing to ride away.

Sam climbed into Henry's cabin and started his engine. Henry flew over the river and landed in a long field covered with great square bales of hay.

'I've come to help Farmer Jones,' he cried. 'I'll carry the hay for you.'

All afternoon he flew from the field to the rick in the farmyard. He carried bales of hay in his cabin. He carried bales of hay dangling between his wheels. The field grew barer and barer, the rick grew higher and higher, and poor Henry grew hotter and hotter. It was almost dark before the last bale was safely stowed on the rick and a big black tarpaulin tied into place to keep it dry.

'Thank you very much,' said Farmer Jones. 'You've saved my hay crop. Here comes the rain.'

Great spots as big as pennies began to splash on Henry's rotors, but he was too tired to fly quickly. By the time he reached the aerodrome he was soaking wet.

'You didn't have a paddle, Henry,' laughed Sam. 'But you look as though you'd had a bathe.'

'Well, at least I'm cool now,' sighed Henry.

'Did you enjoy your day's holiday at the sea-side?' asked Ferdie when Sam had pushed him into the hangar and gone home.

'I didn't get there,' yawned Henry. 'I was a traffic policeman this morning and a hay carter this afternoon.'

'My word, what a busy holiday you've had!' exclaimed Ferdie. 'You've worked harder than I have. I do hope this dreadful storm won't keep us awake again. I'm sure you're very tired.'

But Henry was already fast asleep.

Henry and the hovercraft

THE morning after Henry's busy holiday Sam pushed him out of the hangar as usual.

'My goodness, Henry!' he exclaimed. 'Your cabin floor is covered with hay, and your paint-work is so dirty I could write my name on it.'

'I do look rather grubby,' admitted Henry.

'I must give you a good clean up at once,' said Sam.

He fetched a sponge and a bucket of water, some polish and a duster. He was soon hard at work rubbing and polishing. He did not notice Mr Benson, the aerodrome controller, coming across the grass. With him was a little girl in a blue striped dress.

'Good morning, Sam. Good morning, Henry,' called Mr Benson. 'Spring-cleaning?'

'Henry was very dirty after his hard work yesterday,' explained Sam. 'But I've almost finished. Did you want us?'

'You missed your day at the seaside yesterday,' replied Mr Benson. 'I wondered whether you would take my little daughter Joanna and me today instead.'

'Oh, yes please,' cried Henry.

'This is rather a special trip,' explained Mr Benson. 'I want to go to a really big seaside called Winklesea. They're testing a hovercraft today and I'd like to see what it can do.'

'Hovercraft!' exclaimed Henry. 'Whatever's that?'

'A special new kind of plane,' said Sam. 'It's round like a plate, with a cabin and an engine turret in the middle. It can travel over land and water and it doesn't need a runway.'

'What's so special about it?' asked Henry. 'I can do all those things.'

'It hasn't any wings or rotors,' answered Mr Benson. 'It can carry heavy loads very quickly.'

'I see,' said Henry. But he didn't really.

'I think we're ready now, Mr Benson,' said Sam.

He and Mr Benson and Joanna climbed into Henry's cabin. Sam started his engine and up they went.

It was rather a long way to Winklesea, but Joanna enjoyed every moment of it. Henry waggled his rotors to a ship on the shining silver river and the ship tootled her hooter in reply. An engine driver blew his whistle and waved. The lighthouse keeper sounded a couple of blasts on the fog siren, and presently Henry could see a long pier sticking out into the sea.

'That's Winklesea,' cried Mr Benson. 'There's the fun fair. You can just see the Big Wheel.'

'Do they sit in those little cars and have a ride?' asked Henry, as he passed near the high wheel.

'That's right,' answered Sam.

'The hovercraft is in the car park just beside the fun fair,' said Mr Benson.

Henry dropped neatly down just beside the railings dividing the car park from the fairground. The hovercraft was there too. It *was* a strange-looking plane. Mr Benson and Joanna and Sam climbed out.

'Good morning,' said Henry cheerily. 'I'm Henry. I'm a helicopter.'

'I know,' said the hovercraft, whose name was Horace. 'I've seen lots of helicopters.'

'I've never seen a hovercraft,' said Henry.

'Of course you haven't,' snapped Horace. 'We're very new and special. We can. . . '

But Henry didn't hear what he said next. There was a loud toot-toot. The Big Wheel began to turn. The little cars were loaded with passengers. They all shrieked and shouted as they swung dizzily upwards.

'Oh, I do wish they wouldn't do that,' bellowed Horace crossly. 'They *are* silly.'

'It looked rather fun,' chuckled Henry. 'I wish I could have a ride.'

'Don't be ridiculous!' exclaimed Horace. 'Whoever heard of a helicopter riding on a Big Wheel?'

Just then Mr Benson, Joanna and Sam came back with Horace's pilot Jim. They walked all round the hovercraft. They climbed up into the cabin beside the engine turret and looked at the controls. Then they climbed out again.

'This *is* exciting, Henry,' said Sam. 'The hovercraft is going out on a test.'

Some soldiers came along and cleared everyone out of the way. Jim climbed back into Horace's cabin. All the soldiers climbed aboard, too. There was a loud whining noise, and Horace glided across the beach and then just above the waves.

'He's a splendid craft,' said Mr Benson. 'I'm sure we would find him very useful on our aerodrome. He could share your hangar, Henry.'

'But you've got me,' protested Henry. 'We don't need him.'

'He can carry much heavier loads much quicker,' said Mr Benson.

Henry felt very sad. If Horace came to live on the aerodrome, perhaps he wouldn't be wanted. Besides Horace was such a bad-tempered hovercraft.

Mr Benson and Sam watched Horace's test for a very long time. But Joanna was tired of standing still.

'Can I have an ice-cream, Daddy?' she asked. 'I've brought two shillings of my pocket-money with me.'

'Presently,' said Mr Benson. He went on watching Horace.

'Can I have a ride on the Big Wheel?' asked Joanna.

'In a minute,' replied Mr Benson. 'I want to go to the other end of the car park. We'll get a better view of the test there.'

He and Sam hurried away. Joanna watched them go. Then she turned and walked across to the railings and peeped through. A carload of screaming, excited children plunged down the steep slope of a scenic railway nearby. Joanna looked back, but Mr Benson was still watching the hovercraft. She slipped through a gap in the railings and disappeared.

Henry tried to call Sam, but the noise of the fairground music and the shouting of the children drowned his voice.

When Horace's test was over Sam and Mr Benson walked back. 'It's a wonderful machine —' he began. 'Why, Henry, where's Joanna? I thought she was with you.'

'She squeezed through the railings a long time ago,' said Henry.

'Oh dear!' said Mr Benson. 'We'd better go and look for her.'

He and Sam hurried into the fairground. They went to the ice-cream and the candy-floss stalls, but Joanna wasn't there. They went to the roundabouts and the helter-skelter, but she wasn't there either. They asked at the bumper cars, and the boating lake, but no one had seen a little girl in a blue striped dress. She wasn't in any of the cars that swished down the scenic railway either.

Mr Benson and
Sam hurried back
to where Henry and
Horace waited side
by side.

'Are you sure you
saw Joanna go
through the railings,
Henry?' asked
Mr Benson.

'I know I did,'
declared Henry. 'It
was — Oh!
Goodness gracious!'

'What's the matter?' asked Sam.

'Up there!' gasped Henry. 'Going round on the
Big Wheel!'

Sam and Mr Benson turned round.

'It's Joanna!' shouted Mr Benson.

Alone in one of the cars swinging upwards was a
little girl in a blue striped dress. As they watched
she climbed on to her seat.

'She's unfastened her safety belt,' shouted Sam.

73

'Joanna, sit down!' yelled Mr Benson. But Joanna could not hear him.

Some women on the ground far below started to shriek. The man in charge of the Big Wheel stopped it. All the noise in the fairground hushed, except for Joanna's screams of fright as she clung to the seat at the very top of the wheel.

'If they start the wheel again she'll fall,' gasped Mr Benson. 'Horace, you can fly really fast, will you go up and fetch her?'

'I can't,' muttered Horace. 'I can only fly a little way off the ground.'

'Let me go,' volunteered Henry. 'I can't fly as fast as Horace, but I can go right up above the wheel.'

'Quickly then,' said Mr Benson.

He and Sam climbed into Henry's cabin. As soon as his engine was started Henry shot upwards and in a few moments he was hovering above the Big Wheel.

'Keep very still, Henry,' warned Sam. 'If we frighten Joanna, she'll fall.'

Sam let down the ladder. Mr Benson climbed

carefully down it, trying his best to feel brave.

'Hello, Joanna,' he said gently. 'Henry's come to fetch you.'

'Daddy!' cried Joanna.

Mr Benson lifted her on to the ladder above him. In a few seconds they were safely in Henry's cabin.

Everyone in the fairground cheered. When Henry reached the car park, he was surrounded by an admiring crowd. The ice-cream man gave Joanna a large pink and white cone and a photographer came and took a picture of them all. No one took any notice of Horace.

'Thank you very much for everything, Henry,' said Mr Benson when they were safely back at the aerodrome. 'You are a very clever and useful little helicopter. I don't know what we should have done without you today.'

'Yes,' added Joanna. 'Thank you for bringing me down. I'll never go on a Big Wheel again.'

'That's all right,' said Henry. 'I enjoyed my trip to the big seaside.'

'Will you be getting a hovercraft, Mr Benson?' asked Sam.

'There's no doubt they're very splendid machines,' answered Mr Benson, 'but Henry can do almost everything that a hovercraft can do, and a very great deal that it can't. No, we won't be bringing a hovercraft to share your hangar after all, Henry.'

'Hurrah!' cheered Henry.

Mr Benson and Sam started to laugh.

'Didn't you like Horace?' asked Sam.

'Not very much,' admitted Henry. 'He was a very bad-tempered hovercraft. I know Bumps and Ferdie and Clarence wouldn't have liked him sharing our hangar either.'

Henry's Christmas party

'ONLY two days to Christmas, Henry,' called Sam cheerily as he came into the hangar.

'Is it?' replied Henry. 'I like Christmas. It's fun flying over the big town and seeing all the coloured lights twinkling below us.'

'Talking of lights,' said Sam, 'I've promised my nephew Alan some for his Christmas-tree. I think we'd better go straight away and buy them.'

He pushed Henry out of his hangar and they set off for the big town. In a little while they were over the market square.

'My word!' exclaimed Sam. 'It *is* busy today. I hope there's room for you in the car park.'

Sam managed to squeeze Henry in between a large blue bus and a farm tractor. He was just climbing out of the cabin, when a tall, jolly-looking man, wearing a gold chain around his neck, hurried up.

'Henry and Sam,' he called. 'This *is* lucky. I was just going out to the aerodrome to see you.'

'Good morning, Mr Mayor,' said Sam. 'Can we do anything for you?'

'Not this time,' laughed the mayor. 'We want to do something for you instead.'

'For me?' cried Henry excitedly.

'Yes, for you,' replied the mayor. 'We've been told how you're always helping – policemen, farmers, children, animals, machines and lots more besides.'

'Oh, that was nothing,' said Henry.

'It certainly wasn't nothing,' said the mayor. 'We all think you're the kindest helicopter in the world. We want you to be the special guest at our children's party on Christmas Eve at four o'clock.'

'Me – be the special guest?' squeaked Henry. 'At a Christmas party?'

'Will you bring him, Sam?' asked the mayor. 'We're holding it in the fire-station, so that he can get in through the wide doors.'

'Please let me go, Sam,' pleaded Henry.

'Of course you can,' said Sam.

'Good!' laughed the mayor. 'We're having a conjurer and indoor fireworks too.'

Henry *was* excited. 'I've never seen a conjurer,' he cried, 'and I love fireworks.'

'I've got an idea,' said the mayor. 'Why don't you come early and watch the Christmas-tree being decorated?'

'I'd like to help,' suggested Sam. 'I'm going to buy some fairy lights, so I'll get a few extra decorations.'

'Splendid!' exclaimed the mayor. 'We'll expect you straight after lunch.'

The mayor hurried away. Sam went into the market.

'You are a lucky helicopter,' rumbled the big blue bus.

'I've never been to a Christmas party,' snorted the tractor.

'Especially as special guest,' added the blue bus, full of envy.

'Some machines have all the luck,' grumbled the tractor.

Henry didn't say anything. He knew he was a lucky helicopter.

It was cold in the car park and the wind whistled

round his rotors. He was glad when Sam came hurrying back. He was carrying a large box.

'I've bought the lights, and coloured glass balls, and streamers and a silver star,' he cried. 'Now I think we'd better get back to the hangar. It's going to snow.'

'It won't stop me going to the party, will it?' asked Henry.

'Of course not,' replied Sam. 'You've been out in snow before.'

Sam was quite right. As they reached the aerodrome the first soft flakes were beginning to drift down on to the grass. By Christmas Eve the runways were covered, and the hangar looked just like a giant eskimo's house. It was still snowing hard.

But straight after lunch Sam pushed Henry out of the hangar and started his engine. They flew through the softly falling flakes to the big town and landed in the yard of the fire-station.

The mayor came hurrying out of the big red doors.

'Hello, Henry,' he called. 'I'm afraid we need your help again.'

'What's happened?' asked Sam anxiously.

'Our Christmas-tree hasn't come,' replied the mayor. 'Choo-Choo the engine was bringing a specially large one from the mountain for us, but he hasn't arrived.'

'Oh dear!' exclaimed Henry. 'It's not like Choo-Choo to be late. Something must have happened.'

'We'll go and see straight away,' promised Sam.

He started Henry's engine and up they went. They flew towards the mountains, and presently they were in the narrow valley that led up to Mountain End Station. The snow swirled down so thickly that Henry could hardly see where he was going. The wind tossed him about like a leaf.

'Where is Choo-Choo?' he panted. 'We're nearly at the end of the line.'

'I don't know,' said Sam, peering out of his cabin.

Suddenly Henry saw something. It was a funnel sticking out of a great heap of snow.

'Choo-Choo!' he shouted. 'Whatever's the matter?'

'I'm stuck in a snowdrift,' spluttered Choo-Choo. 'Will you ask the snow-plough to come and dig me out, Henry?'

'Of course I will,' answered Henry. 'Have you got the Christmas-tree for the children's party?'

'Oh yes,' replied William, Choo-Choo's driver. 'It's in a truck next to the guard's van. Will you take it to them, Henry? I'm sorry it's so late.'

William and the guard tied a rope to the Christmas-tree and Sam hauled it up into Henry's cabin. The top stuck out through the door. It looked rather funny, but Henry didn't mind.

'Will you come back and stay with me until I'm dug out, Henry?' pleaded Choo-Choo. 'If the snow gets much deeper, the snow-plough won't be able to find me.'

Henry thought of the Christmas Party. But Choo-Choo was his friend, and he was rather frightened.

'All right,' he sighed. 'I'll come back.'

He flew to the big town as fast as he could go. He asked the station-master to send the snow-plough to dig out Choo-Choo. Then he took the Christmas tree to the fire-station.

'Thank you very much,' said the mayor. 'Come along in and help decorate it. We'll be ready to start the party soon.'

'I'm afraid I won't be able to come to the party

after all,' said Henry. 'I've promised to stay with Choo-Choo until he's dug out.'

'What a pity!' said the mayor. 'We shall miss you, Henry.'

Henry flew straight back to where he had left Choo-Choo. Only the very top of his funnel and his cabin were showing above the snowdrift. Henry hovered above him and whirled his rotors round. The draught blew some of the snow away.

'Thank you, Henry,' spluttered Choo-Choo, glad of his company.

It was two hours before they heard the slow 'chuff-chuff' of the big snow-plough. Henry had managed to keep Choo-Choo's funnel and boiler-top clear, so it didn't take the snow-plough too long to push the drift away and at last Choo-Choo was free.

'Thank you very much, Henry and Sam,' he tooted. 'I'm sure I'd have been buried all Christmas Day without your help.'

'That's all right,' said Henry.

Choo-Choo puffed away down the valley be-hind the big snow-plough.

'We'd better go home,' said Sam. 'I'm afraid it's too late to go to the party.'

They flew slowly back to the aerodrome and Sam pushed Henry into the hangar.

'Happy Christmas, old chap!' he called as he closed the hangar door.

'Did you enjoy the party?' asked Ferdie.

'Was it fun being a special guest?' asked Clarence.

'Did you see the conjurer?' asked Bumps.

'I didn't go,' sighed Henry. 'I —'

But he was interrupted by the opening of the hangar door. Sam hurried in.

'Henry!' he called excitedly. 'Just look who's here?'

Behind Sam trooped the mayor, Father Christmas, two firemen, the conjurer, and lots of children.

'We couldn't let our special guest miss all the fun,' explained the mayor. 'You were too late to come to the party, so we loaded some of it on to a fire tender, and here we are.'

Henry and his friends had a wonderful time.

Father Christmas brought each of them a coloured ball and some streamers off the Christmas-tree to decorate their cabins. Henry had the silver star off the top too. The mayor looped some fairy lights round Henry's rotors, the conjurer pulled rabbits out of a top-hat and the firemen let off the sparkling indoor fireworks. Then the children stood around Henry and sang 'For he's a jolly good fellow.' Henry's little red body glowed with pride and happiness.

'It's getting very late,' said the mayor at last.

'We must go home now. Happy Christmas, Henry.'

'Happy Christmas!' called the boys and girls, Father Christmas, the firemen and the conjurer.

The hangar seemed very quiet after everyone had gone home.

'Wasn't that a lovely party?' sighed Henry. 'I'm glad I went to fetch the Christmas-tree after all.'

'You look rather like one yourself,' grinned Ferdie.

Henry looked up at the red, green and blue lights still glowing round his rotors. Far away in the distance bells started to ring. It was Christmas Day.

'Merry Christmas, everyone,' called Henry happily.

But no one answered him. All the other planes were already fast asleep.

Further adventures with Henry the Helicopter